W9-ARY-603

For Jaime and Erica—S.C.

Text copyright © 1983 by Stephanie Calmenson. Illustrations copyright © 1983 by
Beth Lee Weiner. All rights reserved. Published simultaneously in Canada. Printed in the United States of
America. ISBN: 0-448-14499-9. Library of Congress Catalog Card Number: 83-47680.
1984 PRINTING

The Kindergarten Book

Written by Stephanie Calmenson
Illustrated by Beth Lee Weiner

Publishers • GROSSET & DUNLAP • New York

Contents

See You Later, Alligator

"I don't want to go to school!"
said Owlet to his mother.
"Why not?" asked Mrs. Owl.
"I don't want to leave you."
"But kindergarten is fun," said Mrs. Owl.
"I know you will like it."

7

"I would like to start tomorrow," Owlet said.
"Tomorrow will be a much better
kindergarten-starting day."
"Today is just right," said Mrs. Owl.

8

"It is bright and sunny and as soon as
you finish breakfast we will walk there together."
Owlet had a hard time finishing breakfast.
When he had eaten all he could, he put on his sweater
and walked with his mother to school.

9

"Welcome to Kindergarten Number 1,"
said the teacher.
"Can my mother come to kindergarten with me?"
asked Owlet.
"Kindergarten is only for children," said the teacher.
"But your mother can wait outside if it will
make you feel better."
Owlet said that would make him feel much better,
10   so Mrs. Owl agreed to wait outside.

"What would you like to do first?" asked the teacher.
"I like to draw," Owlet said.
The teacher gave him a box of crayons and paper.
Owlet found a place where he could see his mother.
Then he went to work.
When Owlet finished, he thought his picture looked
very nice.
"Who is that?" asked Rabbit.
"It is my mother," Owlet said.
"She's waiting outside."
"This is my grandfather," said Rabbit.
"He's waiting outside for me, too."

11

Ding-a-ling. The teacher rang a bell.
"Please finish what you're doing and come to the puppet corner."
Owlet put away his crayons and made sure his mother

12   was still outside. Then he went to the teacher.

"I have a friend I'd like you to meet,"
said the teacher. "His name is Alligator.
Alligator has been to kindergarten before.
In fact, he likes it so much he comes back every year.
So if you have any questions, Alligator will
answer them."

"Hello," said Alligator.
"Who would like to ask the first question?"
Rabbit raised his paw.
"What is your favorite toy?" he asked.
"I like to play with blocks," said Alligator.
"Watch me!"
Alligator built a tower with his blocks.
"See?" he said proudly.
"That's a very good tower, Alligator,"
14   said the teacher.

"Now, who else has a question?"
"What do I do if I get hungry?" asked Brown Bear.
"Every day we have milk and cookies,"
Alligator said.
"I like honey," said Brown Bear.
"I'm sure the teacher would bring you bread
and honey if you ask him," said Alligator.

Next Badger went up and whispered in Alligator's ear.
"The bathroom is right over there," Alligator
whispered back. "Can you go by yourself?"
"Yes," said Badger.
16   "Are there any more questions?" asked Alligator.

Everyone was quiet. Finally Owlet asked his question.
"Will you be my friend?" he said.
Alligator gave Owlet a hug.
"I'd like to be your friend," he said.
"Now," said the teacher, "it is time to go home.
But Alligator will be here tomorrow and every day
in case you need to talk to him. So, for now, say,
see you later, Alligator!"
Together Kindergarten Number 1 waved and said
goodbye to Alligator.

17

Owlet ran outside to his mother.
"How was kindergarten?" she asked.
"I liked it!" said Owlet. "And I made a friend."
"Who?" asked Mrs. Owl.
18   "Alligator," Owlet said.

The next morning Owlet finished every bit
of his breakfast.
Then he walked to school with his mother.
"Would you like me to wait outside, Owlet?" she asked.
"No," said Owlet. "I can go to kindergarten all by myself."
Owlet waved to his mother.
"See you later, alligator," he said.

19

Do the Hokey Pokey, Little Chick

Little Chick was in Kindergarten Number 2.
She loved her teacher, Miss Fleagle,
and she had lots of friends.
There was just one problem.
Little Chick couldn't tell her right wing
from her left.

Now, most of the time that was no problem.

Little Chick could answer questions,
because it didn't matter
which wing she waved.

And she could draw pictures,
because she always seemed
to know which wing should
hold her crayon.

She could even put her wing
on her heart and talk to the flag.

Little Chick thought this was funny.
But she always had time to look around and
see which wing everyone else was using,
so she didn't mind.

21

But Little Chick could not do the Hokey Pokey.
When the class went into a circle,
Little Chick's face turned very red.
Little Chick's neck grew very hot.
Then, when Miss Fleagle asked everyone to sing:

22

You put your right wing in,
You take your right wing out,
You put your right wing in,
Then you shake it all about.
You do the Hokey Pokey,
And you turn yourself around.
That's what it's all about!

Little Chick began to cry.

23

Poor Little Chick.
She was crying so hard.
But she wouldn't tell anyone why.
So Little Chick sat off to the side
and watched the others dance.
At nap time, Miss Fleagle came to Little Chick
and whispered in her ear.
Little Chick whispered back.
24   Then the bell rang and everyone went home.

The very next day, right after story hour,
Miss Fleagle said it was time to do the Hokey Pokey.
But this time, before making a circle,
Miss Fleagle asked everyone to line up.

Now when Kindergarten Number 2 sang, Little
Chick's voice was loudest of all.
For on every right wing, Miss Fleagle
had tied a red ribbon.
It wasn't long before the ribbons were forgotten.
But Little Chick never forgot which was her
right wing and which was her left.
And she loved to do the Hokey Pokey.

The Most Fun of All

Monkey was the smallest one in Kindergarten
Number 3.
He was smaller than Lion and Zebra and
much smaller than Elephant and Giraffe.

Whenever the class had to get in a line,
Monkey always had to be first.
The teacher said he could see better that way.

CRAYONS

GAMES

But when he was first on line, Monkey could not
talk and laugh with the others, because
the teacher was always nearby.
Being first on line wasn't the only hard thing
about being small.

At playtime it was hard for Monkey to get his
blocks as high as he wanted.
Someone else always had to help him.
Elephant once whispered in Monkey's ear,
"Being big isn't always fun, either."
But there were times when it seemed to Monkey
that nothing could be as hard as being small.

One day, as Monkey sat reading a book about
a girl as tiny as a thumb, the teacher came to
him and said:
"Sometimes being the smallest is the most fun of all.
Just wait and see."
So Monkey waited for his chance to have
the most fun of all.

And when the teacher told the class about the
kindergarten show, Monkey knew his time had come.
For each class would have to make a special banner
and show it to all the others.
"Of course I'll have to carry the banner,"
Monkey thought.
"It will have to be right at the front of the line,
and I am always first."

But he was very disappointed when the teacher said,
"We'll want everyone to see our beautiful banner,
so it will have to be carried very high."
"I'll be sure to carry the banner, then!" said Giraffe.
And Elephant said, "If I lift my trunk high enough,
maybe I will carry the banner."
Monkey went off to the corner wondering if his turn
for fun would ever really come.

33

On the day of the show, the teacher told
Kindergarten Number 3 to line up.
Monkey walked very slowly.
"Hurry, Monkey," the teacher said.
Kindergarten Number 3 hurried on stage.
When the curtain opened, Monkey was
standing proudly above all the others, singing:

34

We are Kindergarten Number 3,
Here's our banner for you to see.
Short and tall, big and small,
We're the happiest class of all!

35

Who Took the Cookie from the Cookie Jar?

Kindergarten Number 4 was playing the Cookie Jar Game.
It was Gray Goose's turn to sing:
"Who took the cookie from the cookie jar?
Snowy Lamb took the cookie from the cookie jar!"
"Who me?" sang Snowy Lamb.
"Yes, you," answered Gray Goose.
"Couldn't be!" sang Snowy Lamb.
"Then who?" asked Gray Goose.

Snowy Lamb picked Red Rooster.
"Red Rooster took the cookie from
the cookie jar," sang Snowy Lamb.
"Who me?"
"Yes, you!"
"Couldn't be!"
"Then who?"

37

Red Rooster picked Pink Pig to play the game.
"Pink Pig took the cookie from the cookie jar."
But before Pink Pig could answer, there was a
knock at the door of Kindergarten Number 4.
It was Mr. Goat, the school principal.
"I have some special news," Mr. Goat announced.
"Next Monday is visiting day. You are all invited
to bring your mother or father, sister or brother
to school."

"Thank you, Mr. Goat," said
Miss Mallard, the teacher.
"Now it's time for our snack.
Pink Pig, would you give out
the cookies today?"

Carefully Pink Pig put two cookies on every napkin.
But when he got to the last one, there was only
one cookie left.
"Someone took a cookie from the cookie jar!"
cried Pink Pig.
The teacher thought Pink Pig was still playing the game.

40

"Oh, Pink Pig," said Miss Mallard.
"The Cookie Jar Game is over. It's snack time now."
"No, really!" said Pink Pig.
"A cookie is missing!"
"Well, then," said Miss Mallard, "I will have just one cookie today."
Miss Mallard wondered what had happened to that last cookie.
"Oh, well," she thought, "tomorrow I will bring extra cookies—just in case."

41

The next day Kindergarten Number 4 gathered in a circle
for the Cookie Jar Game.
Miss Mallard started:
"Who took the cookie from the cookie jar?" she sang.
"Oh, I took the cookie from the cookie jar!"
answered Mr. Goat. "And I forgot to thank you.
It was delicious!"

ART
Supplies

"Well," said Miss Mallard. "We have two extra
cookies today. Won't you join us for
a snack, Mr. Goat?"
"Thank you," said Mr. Goat.
"I get very hungry sometimes, and I
44   do like cookies!"

From that day on, Mr. Goat spent snack time
with Kindergarten Number 4.
And there were always plenty of cookies
in the cookie jar...
especially on visiting day.